RORY

RORY the Dinosaur
Me and My Dad

Liz Climo

Little, Brown and Company
New York   Boston

This is Rory.

Rory lives on an island with his dad.

He has a lot of energy.

Sometimes too much.

Rory's dad is really fun.

Sometimes he takes Rory fishing...

or to look for seashells.

Rory's dad also loves to read.

But Rory thinks his dad's books are boring.

Now Rory's dad needs some quiet time.

Everything is quiet. Too quiet.

But Rory doesn't want to disturb his dad.

maybe I'll
go on an adventure
all by myself.

So Rory makes his favorite sandwich
(peanut butter and chocolate chip)
and packs a few of his favorite things.

Soon he is on his way to find an adventure,
all by himself.

I'm running
away all
by myself!

Rory walks and walks until he gets to a river.

But he isn't allowed to swim without his dad.

Rory looks around for a way to cross.

Luckily, he notices some rocks

he can use as steps.

I can cross
all by
myself!

Rory walks some more and stops
when he reaches the jungle.

Suddenly, he sees a wild pig
running right toward him!

Rory is scared of wild pigs,
but he wants to be brave.

He lets out a big ROAR...

...and frightens the pig away.

I scared
it all by
myself!

After so much walking, it's time for lunch.

But Rory forgot his coconut water.

aw, man.
dad usually
packs my drink
for me.

Just as Rory considers skipping lunch (after all,
a peanut butter and chocolate chip sandwich
just isn't the same without a drink),

a coconut falls from the tree above him
and breaks in half.

I found
something
to drink
all by myself!

After lunch, it begins to rain.

Rory looks everywhere for shelter,

but he can't find anything to keep him dry.

Suddenly, the rain stops right where he's standing.

The storm passes, and the sun comes out.

A magnificent rainbow stretches across the sky.

Rory loves rainbows!
His dad always helps him
find one after a storm.

dad! look!
I found a
rainbow
all by myself!

But then Rory remembers—his dad isn't there.

He's all the way back home.

So Rory decides to run back and get him.

Rory tells his dad all about his journey.

"But I'll wait a while before
I leave home again," Rory says.
"I don't want you to miss me too much."

"That sounds like a good plan," says Rory's dad.

Together they head back to the tree house...

...and dream of new adventures.

for
marlow

About This Book

The illustrations for this book were done with digital magic. The text was set in CG Schneidler, and the display type was hand-lettered by the author. This book was edited by Connie Hsu and designed by Phil Caminiti with art direction by Patti Ann Harris. The production was supervised by Erika Schwartz, and the production editor was Christine Ma.

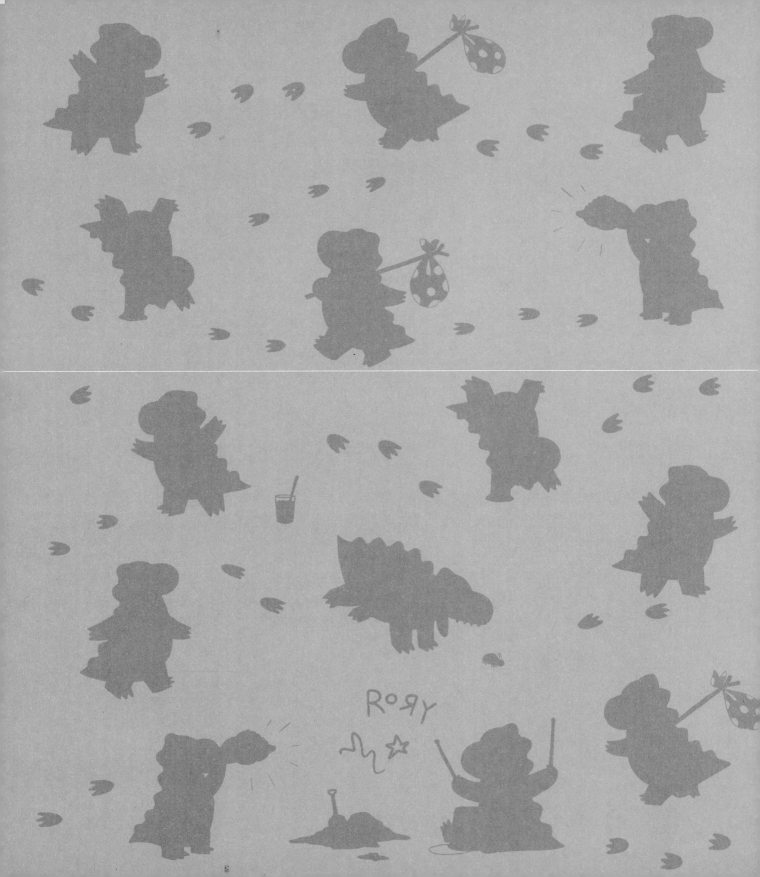